I Don't Like Gloria!

For Alfie and Charlie
        K. U.

For Ruth, Lowell, and Cara,
with love
        M. C.

Text copyright © 2007 by Kaye Umansky
Illustrations copyright © by 2007 Margaret Chamberlain

First U.S. edition 2007

Library of Congress Cataloging-in-Publication Data
Umansky, Kaye.
I don't like Gloria! / Kaye Umansky ; illustrated by Margaret Chamberlain. —
1st U.S. ed.
p.   cm
Summary: The family dog tries to cope with the arrival of a new pet.
ISBN-10: 0-7636-3202-3
ISBN-13: 978-0-7636-3202-1
[1. Dogs—Fiction. 2. Cats—Fiction.   3. Pets—Fiction.]
I. Chamberlain, Margaret, ill. II. Title. III. Title: I don't like Gloria!
PZ7.U363Iag 2007
[E]—dc22   2006041644

10 9 8 7 6 5 4 3 2 1

Printed in Singapore

This book was typeset in Gill Sans.
The illustrations were done in pencil and digitally colored.

Candlewick Press
2067 Massachusetts Avenue
Cambridge, Massachusetts 02140

visit us at www.candlewick.com

I Don't Like Gloria!

Kaye Umansky   illustrated by Margaret Chamberlain

CANDLEWICK PRESS
CAMBRIDGE, MASSACHUSETTS

I don't like Gloria.
She's a cat.
She's going to live with us.

Nobody asked me.

The first thing she did
was eat out of my bowl.

MY bowl.

She has her own bowl.
It says GLORIA on it.
Mine says CALVIN.

Can't she read?

When I growled at her,
I got yelled at.

Is that fair?

I don't like

Gloria.

Gloria has taken over the house!
She even sleeps in my basket.

On my special cushion.

Nobody remembered my walk today.

They were too busy with Gloria.

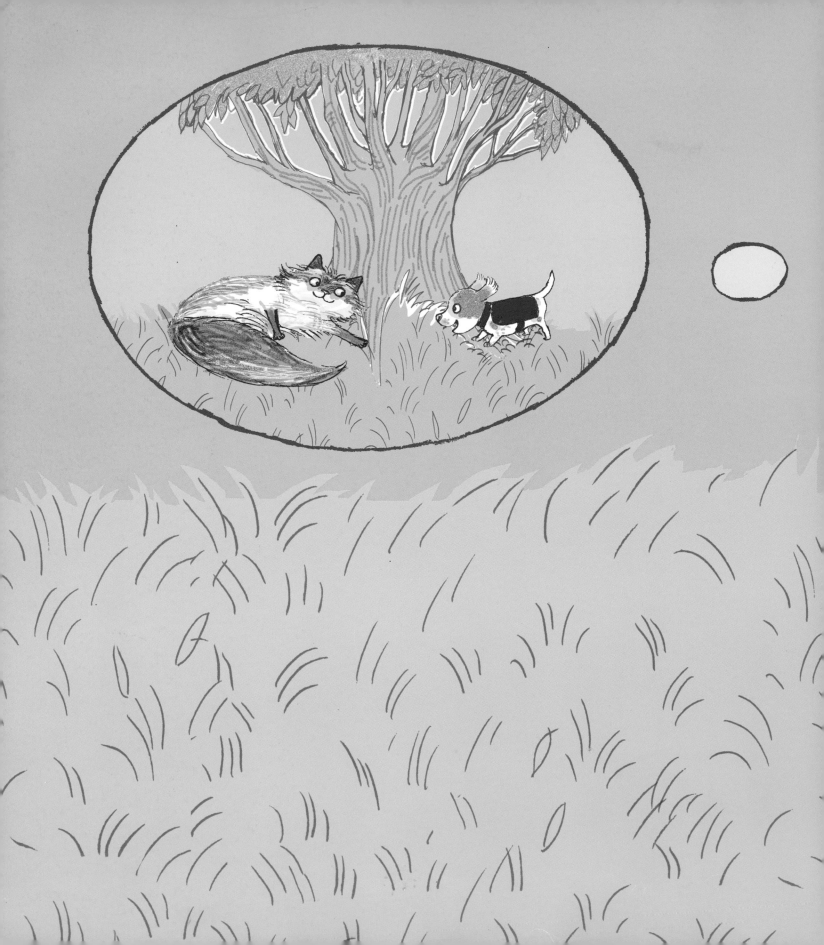

Gloria's taken over the yard, too!
MY yard. I tried chasing her
up a tree, but she wouldn't budge.

I felt silly.

I got yelled at for barking.

Can you believe it?

I Really
don't like
GLORIA!

Hey, what's this?

When I go to investigate,
I'm shooed away.
When Gloria goes to investigate,
she's shooed away, too!

But we saw
it anyway.

His name is Jeffrey.
He's going to live with us.

Now, nobody's paying any attention to me OR Gloria.

They're too busy
with Jeffrey.

I still don't like Gloria,
and Gloria doesn't like me.

But at least we agree on one thing.

We REALLY
don't like Jeffrey!